SPARTAN &
The Green Egg

— A TRIP TO THE RAINFOREST —

Nabila Khashoggi

ILLUSTRATED BY MANUEL CADAG

BOOK 1

Spartan & The Green Egg

www.spartanandthegreenegg.com

Cover and interior illustrations by Manuel Cadag
Cover and interior designer by Ted Ruybal
Story structure and editor: Danny Daggenhurst
Copyeditor: Joan Warschauer
Consultant: Deborah Kanafani Samiha Dauk

ISBN-13 978-0-6154326-6-3 • ISBN-10: 0-6154326-6-2
LCCN:2012952839 • Registration number TXu 1-789927
BISG: JUV008000: Junenile Fiction/Comics & Graphic Novels/General

Printed in China

Spartan & The Green Egg

Full Cycle
PUBLICATIONS

Quality reading and entertainment

www.fullcyclepublications.com

Part of the proceeds of the sale of this book go to
The Children for Peace ONLUS. www.thechildrenforpeace.org

For
Jim, Spartan, Layth . . .
&
all the other adventurers
around the world.

2

It's pretty heavy, what's the book about?

Well' that's just it, I read the first chapter last night. You'll never guess, not in a hundred years..

Oh come on Spartan please tell us now, you know how I can't stand being made to wait for a surprise.

All right, this book will show us how to contact aliens from Outer Space!

The secret is very simple, but that's what makes it so difficult at the same time.

The book says that what we have to do is to use our minds. When the book was written long ago, they didn't even have radios and satellites and stuff like that. But even now, the most powerful machines can't reach out far enough to make contact with aliens.

BUT, *minds made the machines, so minds are more powerful than machines!* The book tells us how to use our minds directly, without needing the machines.

Yes, but how DO we use our minds? I mean, I'm having enough difficulty with my geometry and science, let alone with something as far out as making contact with aliens.

Ha! Ha! Ha!

Well, that's just it Max... We have to use the power of our imaginations and the book tells us how.

What we do is this. We each imagine a bright golden light coming from our heads and together making a bow and a single arrow. Then we imagine shooting this golden arrow made up of 'Mind Light', into outer space, and it will immediately make contact with the minds of aliens!

Mmm...

6

OK, I accept the idea of imagination, most of my math comes to me without really thinking about it, kinda like imagining it, but...

Hullo, what's this?

Hello!

!!??!!

Yes it is me, the Egg talking. You are hearing me in your minds because that's how we can communicate from so far away. It's been a long time since I last spoke to members of the human race. The last one I spoke to, thousands of years ago, were Greeks, children like you, who managed to send their message across the vast distances of space. In return I came to your planet. Those children...

Who are you?

Yeah, and where are you from? What star system?

Whoah! One question at a time! As I was saying, it was children just like you who were last able to make contact with us. Like you, they had pure hearts and minds, so strong that their Mind's Light crossed space and reach my planet.

What shall we call you?

Egg will be fine.

Wow this is amazing!

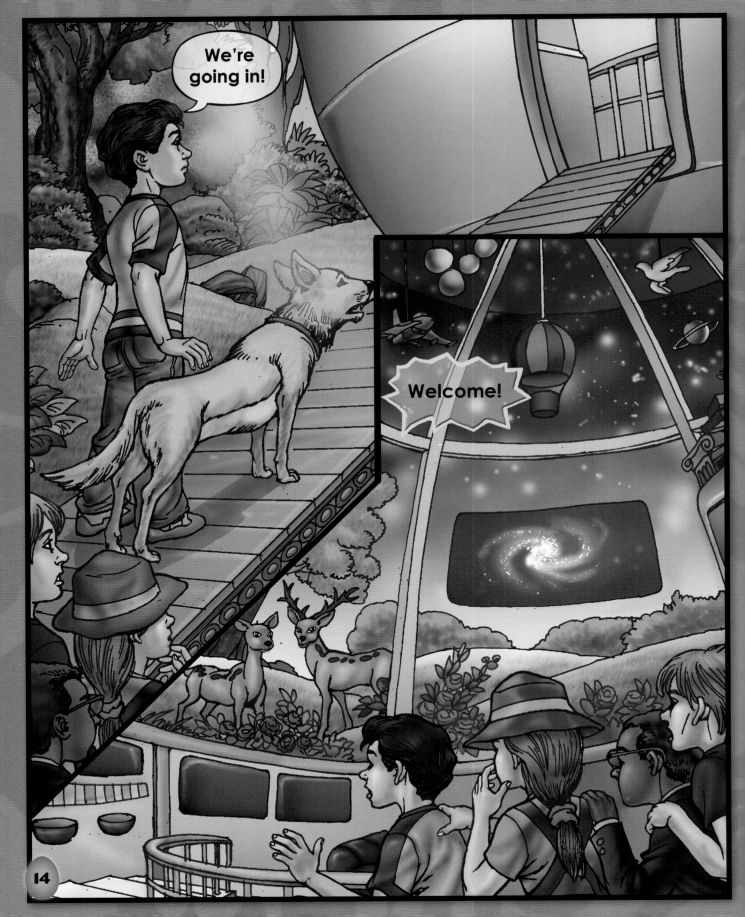

Spartan! where are we? What were you thinking?

Jaguars, anacondas and giant anteaters! I think that Egg must have brought us to the Amazon.

Wow! The Amazon!

What do you know of the Amazon, Max?

What's that on your head?

I wanted to look up an answer and this headset appeared! It's a mini computer!

The Amazon is a huge forest in South America. It's a rain forest, which means that it rains a lot and there are all sorts' trees and plants. The trees and plants breathe IN the old air from cars and trucks and factories, you know stuff that we don't like to breathe and then they breathe OUT oxygen, which is the fresh stuff that we like to breathe!

So you mean that the rain forest is a bit like a big lung machine?

Yes.

Get this! The air that we breathe out from our lungs is also what the trees and plants like to breathe in! We breathe in what the trees breathe out and the trees breathe in what we breathe out!

Oh Max! That's a lot of information!

Magic back packs!

Egg has disappeared!

No I haven't! I am here in Spartan's head set. Did you think that you would leave ME all alone in the forest while you went exploring? You'll find these head sets handy!

We really are in the Amazon jungle!

Careful Grimm or you'll get nipped!

It's hot!

Well this must be a path. Let's see where it takes us.

Oh yeah, and what if this is one of those paths where jaguars hide, waiting for lunch to come along, what then eh?

21

Look! They could have chewed us up!

Who warned us?

What do you think you are doing running around making so much noise?! Look what you have done, you've scared away our fishes!

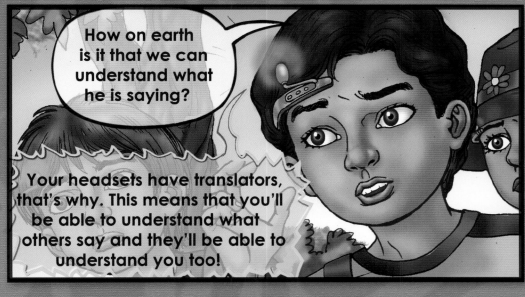

How on earth is it that we can understand what he is saying?

Your headsets have translators, that's why. This means that you'll be able to understand what others say and they'll be able to understand you too!

24

Hello! Nice to meet you.

There's a bridge behind the next bend in the river, you can cross safely there.

So exactly what kind of magicians are you then?

Beginners!

26

29

Yikes!

SPLASSH!

Great dive, Spartan. 10 out of 10 I would say.

Make sure you don't forget anything and we will head back to our village..

We share most things in life. We work, hunt and fish together. Our houses are called Malocas and they are made mainly of mud, tree bark, palm leaves and stone. Entire families, parents, grandparents, brothers, sisters, uncles, cousins can live in the same house. Sharing is key to survival from materials such as tree bark and palm leave fronds.

Follow us we will take you to where the Shaman lives.

This is our Shaman, he is very wise.

Welcome to our village, I hope that my young friend Juma is looking after you well. Stay a while with us here; there is much that you can learn from us and we from you.

You have so many pots.

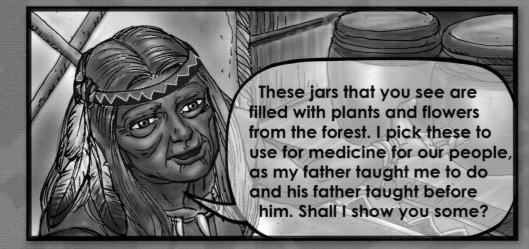

These jars that you see are filled with plants and flowers from the forest. I pick these to use for medicine for our people, as my father taught me to do and his father taught before him. Shall I show you some?

Native Amazonians have lived in the forests for thousands of years, there are many different tribes spread along the Amazons, we have our own way of life in harmony with nature.

He looks important.

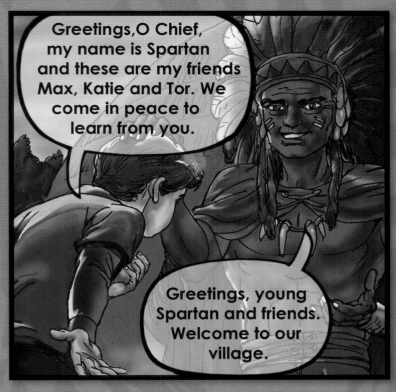

Greetings, O Chief, my name is Spartan and these are my friends Max, Katie and Tor. We come in peace to learn from you.

Greetings, young Spartan and friends. Welcome to our village.

This is delicious!

Boy that was a terrible nightmare!

What a lovely place this is! Could it really be destroyed so easily?

Spartan, I had the most terrible dream...

I did too. I dreamed that the whole forest was being cut down by loggers, and the animals and plants..

...died! We had the same dream?

It was the Shaman, he's done it before. It's part of his magical powers. Perhaps he thinks that you can help us in some way.

I think that we can. Egg, why are the trees being cut down and what can we do to stop it?

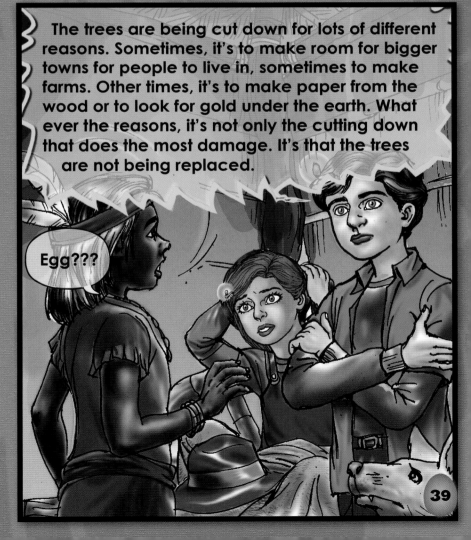

The trees are being cut down for lots of different reasons. Sometimes, it's to make room for bigger towns for people to live in, sometimes to make farms. Other times, it's to make paper from the wood or to look for gold under the earth. What ever the reasons, it's not only the cutting down that does the most damage. It's that the trees are not being replaced.

Egg???

What do you mean 'replaced'? How can you replace a tree once you've cut it down?

Easy. All you have to do is to plant a new seed for every tree that you cut down and then the forest will never get smaller!

That's right Katie. You just have to make sure that you replant the same type of tree that you've cut down, also you have to make sure that you don't cut again in the same place until the trees are big enough.

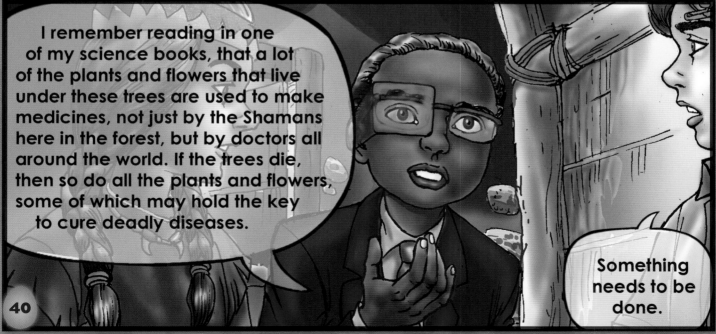

I remember reading in one of my science books, that a lot of the plants and flowers that live under these trees are used to make medicines, not just by the Shamans here in the forest, but by doctors all around the world. If the trees die, then so do all the plants and flowers, some of which may hold the key to cure deadly diseases.

Something needs to be done.

We have arrived in the forest behind the camp of the loggers.

They can't see us, I've put a shield around us that makes us invisible.

Lunch time!

I am starved.

Me too, that was hard work we got lots more trees down today!

You did a great job today, you have earned yourselves a bonus.

47

How did this happen???

LOOK! The crane is up in the tree!

KZZZZZZT!

Great Spirit of the Forest, we are sorry for the harm that we have caused. We will, from today on, make sure that we replant one new tree for every tree that we cut down, and will protect the plants and flowers too. We don't want our children to inherit a desert! We shall make sure that your message is passed on to all other loggers.

Well, that's good start.

Goodbye Great Spirit of the Forest!

We've won!

They were fooled by Egg's giant.

At least these loggers will try protect the forest as their own home, just as we Indians have done for thousands of years. Thank you my friends!

Thank you, O Egg, for your magic Giant!

Next time, I think the super hero should look like me!

Whoooossshh

Home sweet home!

Where's Egg?

57

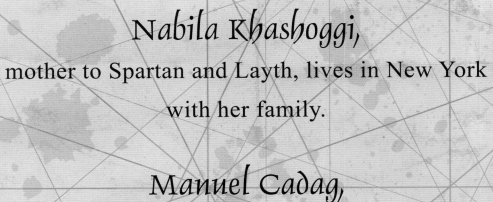

Nabila Khashoggi,

mother to Spartan and Layth, lives in New York
with her family.

Manuel Cadag,

is an artist and illustrator who lives
in the Philippines.